# Aesop's Fun

# The Tortoise and the Hare RETOLD

## Eric Braun

BLACK RABBIT BOOKS

Hi Jinx is published by Black Rabbit Books
P.O. Box 3263, Mankato, Minnesota, 56002.
www.blackrabbitbooks.com
Copyright © 2021 Black Rabbit Books

Jen Besel, editor; Michael Sellner, interior designer;
Catherine Cates, cover designer; Omay Ayres,
photo researcher

Library of Congress Cataloging-in-Publication Data
Names: Braun, Eric, author. | Aesop.
Title: The tortoise and the hare retold / by Eric Braun.
Description: Mankato, Minnesota : Black Rabbit Books, [2021] |
Series: Hi jinx. Aesop's funny fables | Includes bibliographical references. |
Audience: Ages 8-12. | Audience: Grades 4-6. | Summary: Two retellings
(one modern, one traditional) of the classic fable that follows the events
of the famous race between the boastful hare and the persevering tortoise.
Includes discussion questions and examines the moral of the fable.
Identifiers: LCCN 2019044627 (print) | LCCN 2019044628 (ebook) |
ISBN 9781623103064 (hardcover) | ISBN 9781644664025 (paperback) |
ISBN 9781623104009 (ebook)
Subjects: CYAC: Fables. | Folklore.
Classification: LCC PZ8.2.B66 To 2021  (print) | LCC PZ8.2.B66  (ebook) |
DDC 398.2—dc23
LC record available at https://lccn.loc.gov/2019044627
LC ebook record available at
https://lccn.loc.gov/2019044628


Printed in the United States. 1/20

## Image Credits

# CONTENTS

# Chapter 1

# Story Time!

One day, a tortoise was walking through the forest. From behind, he heard a sound. Thump! Thump! Soon, a hare zoomed up.

"You're so slow!" the hare said to the tortoise. "When you cross the street, you get a parking ticket!"

"Well ..." the tortoise responded slowly.

"You're so slow! It takes you an hour to fall down!"

The hare was on a roll with the **slowpoke** jokes. He didn't care about the tortoise's feelings. "You're so slow! You'd get run over by a parked car!" he said.

"Not fair," said the tortoise. "You know I have to carry my shell."

"Michelle?" asked the hare. "Who's Michelle?"

"My shell," repeated the tortoise, but the hare was too busy laughing at his own joke.

"Your shadow is faster than you,"
the hare said. He was on fire with
the jokes. "Dust settles on you when
you run. When you run a race, the snail
gives you a head start!"

Well, the snail IS a fast little fella.

START

The tortoise was tired of listening to the **cocky** hare. He knew he wasn't fast, but he was smart. "Do you want to race?" he asked the hare.

The hare laughed even harder at that. "You want to race me? Don't you know I'm the fastest around? I'm faster than the Internet. I travel faster than bad news."

The tortoise simply nodded. So the two set up the course and lined up for a race.

Ready!
Set! Go!

The hare dashed out to a big lead. He yelled back to the tortoise. "Did you forget how fast I am? Maybe this will **jog** your memory!" And then he sped away.

The tortoise ran as fast as he could. He passed three blades of grass in less than 10 minutes. "Wheeee!" he said. Tears peeled back from his eyes.

Meanwhile, the hare was almost to the finish. He thought it would be funny to stop and nap. He could waste all the time he wanted and still win. That would be hilarious.

The hare laid down for a nap. He snored and snored and snored.

The tortoise ran and ran and ran.

Eventually, the tortoise passed the sleeping hare. "I'm in the lead! And I'm carrying my house on my back!"

The tortoise was almost to the finish line. Suddenly, the hare woke up.

"No fair!" he yelled when he saw the tortoise.

15

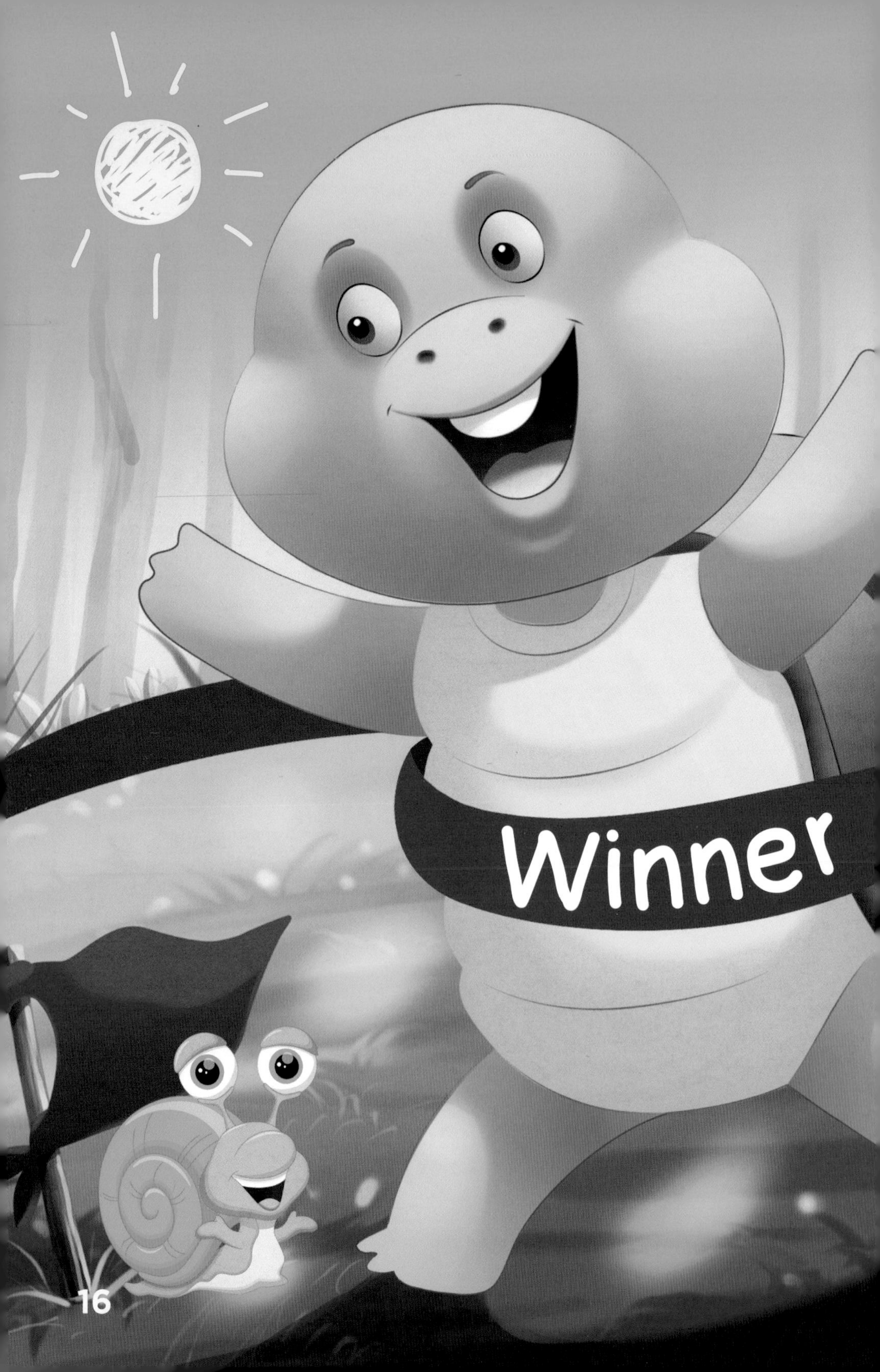
Winner

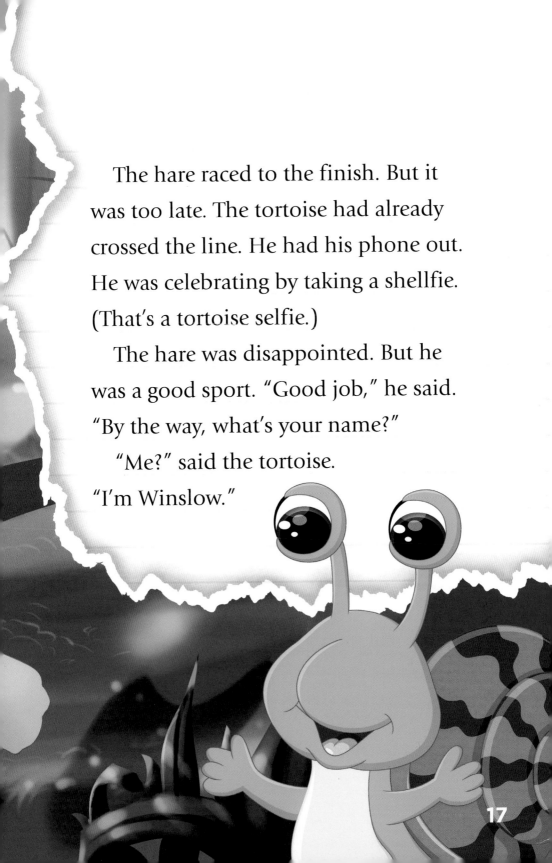

The hare raced to the finish. But it was too late. The tortoise had already crossed the line. He had his phone out. He was celebrating by taking a shellfie. (That's a tortoise selfie.)

The hare was disappointed. But he was a good sport. "Good job," he said. "By the way, what's your name?"

"Me?" said the tortoise. "I'm Winslow."

17

# Chapter 2

# Aesop's Fable

The story of the tortoise and the hare is an old one. This tale is one of Aesop's **fables**. Aesop was a **legendary** storyteller. Some researchers think Aesop was a slave who lived in **ancient** Greece. Other researchers say Aesop wasn't a real person. But over the years, he got credit for writing stories that teach **morals**.

This version of the story is different from the original. It has jokes and silly images. But the moral stayed the same. Compare this version with Aesop's original story.

# The Hare and the Tortoise

A hare was making fun of the tortoise one day for being so slow.

"Do you ever get anywhere?" he asked with a mocking laugh.

"Yes," replied the tortoise, "and I get there sooner than you think. I'll run you a race and prove it."

The hare was much amused at the idea of running a race with the tortoise, but for the fun of the thing he agreed. So the fox, who had **consented** to act as a judge, marked the distance and started the runners off.

The hare was soon far out of sight, and to make the tortoise feel very deeply how ridiculous it was for him to try to race with a hare, he lay down beside the course to take a nap until the tortoise could catch up.

The tortoise meanwhile kept going slowly but steadily, and, after a time, passed the place where the hare was sleeping. But the hare slept on very peacefully; and when at last he did wake up, the tortoise was near the goal.

The hare now ran his swiftest, but he could not overtake the tortoise in time.

*The race is not always to the swift.*

# Chapter 3
## Get in on the Hi Jinx

Aesop gave a moral for this fable. He said, "The race is not always to the swift." Another way of putting it is, "Slow and steady wins the race."

You can apply this to your own life. Don't rush through your homework. Take the time to do it the right way, even if it takes a little longer. That extra effort will pay off. Maybe you want to be great at something, like playing an instrument. Practice a little every day. Building skills isn't a fast process. But if you keep going, you'll get there!

# Take It One Step More

1. Is it ever OK to tease someone? Why or why not?

2. Why do you think the tortoise wanted to race when he knew the hare was faster?

3. Have you ever rushed to finish something that you should have taken your time with? What happened?

# LEARN MORE

## GLOSSARY

**ancient** (AYN-shunt)—from a time long ago

**cocky** (KAH-kee)—very sure of oneself

**consent** (kun-SENT)—to agree to do something

**fable** (FAY-buhl)—a story intended to share a useful truth

**jog** (JAHG)—to make more alert; it also means a slow run.

**legendary** (LEH-juhn-dahr-ee)—relating to a story from the past that cannot be proven true

**moral** (MOR-uhl)—a lesson that is learned from a story or an experience

**slowpoke** (SLOH-pohk)—a very slow person

## BOOKS

**Loewen, Nancy.** *The Tortoise and the Hare, Narrated by the Silly but Truthful Tortoise.* The Other Side of the Fable. North Mankato, MN: Picture Window Books, 2019.

**Miller, Connie Colwell.** *Henry's Track and Field Day: The Tortoise and the Hare Remixed.* Aesop's Fables Remixed. Mankato, MN: Amicus Illustrated, 2017.

**St. Pierre, Todd-Michael.** *Thibodeaux Turtle and Boudreaux Bunny: The Tortoise and the Hare with a Louisiana Twist.* Gretna, LA: Pelican Publishing Company, 2019.

## WEBSITES

Library of Congress Aesop Fables
**www.read.gov/aesop/001.html**

The Tortoise and the Hare
**www.youtube.com/watch?v=QzoQcIYhnqo**